SHOWDOWN

AT

WAMEGO FALLS

A Clay Jared Western

R. Annan

Showdown at Wamego Falls
Copyright 2016 by R. Annan
E. 1.1
WGA Reg. #: R31680

Photography © L. Annan
Editor: Karren Doll Tolliver
Author's Portrait by Hazel Tertsakian

One Vision Publishing
ISBN: 978-1-942338-48-2 (eBook)
ISBN: 978-1-942338-47-5 (Print)

OTHER WESTERN BOOKS BY R. ANNAN

Fight for the Lazy M
The Red Bandana
The Gunfighter in Winter
Long Ride to Hell's Kitchen
Owl Hawks
Gunfight at Barfield Springs
Shootout at Sanctuary City
Last Days of a Gunfighter
Red Bandana
Copperhead Moon
Cowboys of the Box R
Prisoners of Brimstone Pass
Range War in C Minor
Devil Wind

Dedication

To the Annan Clan of Texas

1.

On a cold, snowy evening in December, Clay Jared rode up to the top of a hill and stopped to look down at a small stagecoach swing station a hundred yards below.

At first glance everything looked normal. On second glance, not so much.

First of all, the corral was empty even though there should have been a fresh team of horses waiting for the next stagecoach due to come in. Second, there were three horses tied in a stand of pine trees behind the station. No one coming along the road would see them, but, from where he sat, Jared could.

He wondered why they were hidden there.

Jared sat in the saddle and watched as a gust of wind spiraled up the road. It raised a snow ghost and flung it at the station door, then rose over the roof to the brick chimney and played with the smoke coming out. The smoke bent and shuddered and faded out of sight.

Jared's horse pounded the frozen ground, anxious to move. The cowboy leaned over and patted its neck.

"Okay, pal," he chuckled. "Let's go."

Jared held the reins in his left hand and dropped his right one down by his Colt.

The horse moved quickly down the long slope, crossed the hardpan road and stopped at the hitching rail. Without taking his eyes off the station door, Jared eased out of the saddle onto the ground. He quietly tied onto the rail, hoping the wind would cover any noise he was making.

Pulling the collar of his mackinaw up around his neck and his hat low, Jared opened the station door and stepped in.

Like most swing stations, it had little to see except a few small, square, worn wooden tables with chairs, a fireplace, and a crude plank bar. A fire blazed in the fireplace. A single oil lamp hung from a roof beam. In the back, a short hallway led to two rooms.

Two men in black, wide-brimmed hats and long, black winter coats stood drinking together at the bar near the door. They pretended to ignore Jared as he walked past them.

When the barman gave him a worried look, Jared took that as a signal that something was wrong. He looked around. There was no one else, just the two men, the barman, and himself in the station.

Jared wondered why they had tied their horses out back, and why there were three horses out there in the pines instead of two.

He walked over to the fireplace to warm his hands, undecided as to what to do. He could move on, but the next town was a long way off. He'd never make it in this storm. Jared decided to play the cards he was dealt.

"It's bad out there," Jared said.

The man nearest to him at the bar slowly turned his face to Jared. His wide-brimmed hat rode low on his head, hiding all but his mouth.

"Is it?" the man asked in a hard, grainy voice.

"Yeah," Jared said, "snowing hard."

Jared reached into his shirt pocket for the makings of a cigarette. The man watched his every move as he rolled and lit it. Jared decided to buy a drink to ward off the cold. He was chilled to the bone.

Jared walked to the far end of the bar, took a double eagle from his pocket, and sent it skittering along the plank towards the barman. It never got there. The man in black snatched it up and sent it spinning back at Jared.

"The bar is closed, friend," the man said calmly.

His partner took a sip of his whiskey and said, "See? I told ya we shoulda locked the damn door."

"Hell, who woulda thought some dumb-assed cowboy would be out in this kinda stuff?"

At that moment Jared knew something was very screwed up. He had two choices, run scared or bluff it out. Neither seemed good options now.

"He didn't say it," Jared said, nodding at the barman. "He has to say it."

"I'm saying it, cowboy," the man growled. "Now get back on your horse and ride out."

"I'll think about it after I get my drink," Jared said coolly.

Suddenly the barman spoke up.

"I'm sorry, mister, the bar is closed."

"I see," Jared replied. "Did they threaten to kill you?"

"You're askin' for trouble, cowboy," the taller man said. He stepped away from the bar and put his hand down by his gun.

"Are you trouble?" Jared asked. "I took you for a carpetbagger, asshole!"

Jared dropped to his knees and to the left, using the end of the bar as a shield. Two bullets tore into the plank above his head as he fanned off two quick shots. They were close, easy targets and his first shot hit the tall man in the chest. He drilled the short man in the stomach.

There was an ear-shattering boom as the barman drew and fired his double-barreled shotgun, hitting both targets in the chest at close range and sending their bodies flying across the room, crashing into the tables.

Gun smoke curled up towards the oil lamps on an updraft. Jared quickly reloaded. The barman laid the shotgun on the bar and poured two shots of whiskey. His hands shook badly. They drank two quick shots.

"It's on the house," the barman said.

Jared got a good look at him. He was about twenty. He looked more like a bank teller than a barman.

"Who were they?" Jared asked.

"Part of the Jace Ramsey gang."

"Ramsey?"

"Yeah."

"He's in prison, ain't he?" Jared asked.

"He's being moved to Leavenworth for safekeeping."

"Didn't he rob the Perryville Cattlemen's Savings and Loan Bank? Got away with seventy-five thousand?"

"Yeah, and they never got it back. Ramsey hid it someplace before they caught him a week later at a cathouse in Belcher's Flats," the barman said. "His stage is supposed to pull in here for a change of horses."

"There aren't any."

"Yeah, I know. The tall guy scattered them. I don't know why."

"I guess he thought it was a good thing to do," Jared said. "Some of these guys aren't so smart."

"I guess not. By the way, my name is Ted Lowry."

"I'm Clay Jared. Glad to meet you, Lowry."

Suddenly they heard noise out on the road.

"That must be them," Lowry said.

The sound grew louder until it stopped in front of the swing station door.

2.

The stage pulled up with a thunder of hoof beats and screeched to a stop outside the door. Jared could hear voices. There were various sounds of people unloading and stamping their feet. Then came swearing and complaining about the weather. Finally, the door burst open.

A short, stocky man wearing a gray wool coat came in. His coat was purposely opened in front to flaunt a sheriff's badge. He wore a black Stetson pulled low on his forehead. He was perhaps fifty years old and had long, brown hair. He had a large nose, small, beady eyes, and razor-thin lips. His face was flushed as if from too much drinking in the past.

A tall, broad-shouldered man of about forty dressed in a prison uniform came in behind the sheriff. He was very handsome in a cruel, roguish sort of way but sad about the eyes, which were a deep blue. He wore prison work shoes on his feet and was handcuffed and shackled.

He stood looking around, smiling.

A deputy carrying a rifle and wearing a gun followed the prisoner. He was tall and lean and wore a mackinaw and hat. Behind him came the stage driver wearing a buffalo-skin coat and hat.

They all stopped to look at the two bodies lying askew near the far wall in a pool of blood.

"What the hell happened here?" the sheriff asked.

The barman gave a quick, short version of what had happened.

The sheriff looked at the prisoner and chuckled. "So much for your rescue attempt, Ramsey."

The prisoner shrugged and shuffled over to the fireplace.

The deputy and the driver also went to warm themselves, ordering a whiskey as they went past the bar.

The sheriff gave Jared the once-over, went to the bar, and ordered a whiskey. Lowry quickly poured him one.

"I'm Sheriff Dan Noble," he said, directing his words at Jared and Lowry. "Thet's my prisoner. You all stay away from him, understand?" Jared and Lowry nodded. The sheriff centered his attention on Lowry. "You got anything ta eat?"

Lowry reached under the bar and brought up a jar of pickled eggs and another with cucumbers in brine. He added a bowl of hardtack and a bowl of jerky. The sheriff dug in. The deputy and the driver came over for their drinks and some food, too, leaving Ramsey alone by the fire.

The sheriff kept staring at Jared.

"You ever rob a bank?"

"No, can't say as I have, Sheriff," Jared said, resisting the urge to laugh.

"What's yer name, mister?"

"Jared, Clay Jared."

"You look familiar, Jared. We haven't crossed paths, have we?"

"No, sir," Jared replied.

The deputy and the driver got a bottle of whiskey, two glasses and a deck of cards and then went over to a table and sat down. Jared took two eggs and a slice of beef jerky over to the fireplace and handed them to Jace Ramsey.

"Thanks, friend," Ramsey said.

Just as the prisoner started to eat, Noble rushed over and slapped the food out of Ramsey's hands. He shoved a finger in Jared's face.

"I said ta stay away from the prisoner!" the sheriff growled. "I got another set of bracelets if ya wanna wear 'em."

The sheriff followed Jared as he walked back to the bar.

"You, barman," he said to Lowry, "get yer helper an' take those two bodies outside. While yer out there, change the horses. We gotta git moving fer Leavenworth."

"I can't," Ted Lowry said. "I don't have a helper and there aren't any horses. One of them yokels let the horses loose. They might be back by morning, if you're lucky."

"Jesus!" the sheriff said. "Thet's the dumbest thing I ever heard. No wonder they're layin' on the floor dead as doornails."

The sheriff pointed at Jared.

"You help him drag them bodies outside before they start ta stinkin' up the place."

Lowry grabbed his coat from a peg on the wall and walked around the bar.

One by one he and Jared carried the two bodies outside and around to the back. Lowry noticed the three horses tied up in the pines.

"What about them?"

"We'll feed and water 'em with the stagecoach horses," Jared said. "And I gotta take care of my own bronc, too. He's tired, thirsty and hungry."

"Alright."

Lowry led Jared into the grain and water shack near the corral. They each carried a pail of oats and a pail of water to the three outlaw horses.

"We'll have to feed the two coach horses, too," Lowry said. "Will you give me a hand?"

"Sure," Jared shouted against the wind. It was snowing hard.

The barman got up on the driver's seat and drove the coach around the back to the grain shed. He and Jared fed and watered the horses and laid blankets over their backs. By the time they were finished it was snowing harder than before. They had to bend over and fight the wind. Darkness was settling in.

3.

The whole thing fascinated Jared. He had heard about both men.

Jace Ramsey had earned a reputation in his early days as a Confederate bushwhacker. After several years of that, he ditched the politics and turned to the more lucrative profession of robbing trains and banks. He was pretty good at it and managed to dodge the noose for a long time.

Then, six months ago, he robbed the Perryville Cattlemen's Savings and Loan Bank of seventy-five thousand dollars and disappeared. The bank owner, J. D. Dalgren, hired the Pinkerton Agency, and three months later Ramsey was arrested in a hotel in Belcher's Flats, in the Kansas badlands.

Sheriff Dan "Bulldog" Noble had a reputation equal to Ramsey's. He was best known as a regulator for a large cattle combine in Lawrence, south of Kansas City. His fame came from tracking down and hanging a band of fifteen cattle rustlers. Noble was noted for being a dedicated lawman who never gave up the hunt. No matter how long it took, Bulldog Noble always got his man. Train robbers and bank robbers alike feared him.

Noble's trusty deputy, Ed Weber, was equal to his master and had been at his side through hell and high water, thick and thin, for as long as anyone could remember. Weber was known for his sadistic mean streak. He would strike without warning and some people called him "Snake Face" Weber.

Jared had heard of these two lawmen, and now here he was in the same room with the two living legends.

As he and Lowry brought in extra wood for the fire, Jared glanced at the table where Weber and the coach driver, a man called Val, were playing cards. Weber didn't look too happy. He was losing money to the coach driver and didn't like it.

While Jared stoked up the fire, Ramsey pulled a chair up close to the flames. His one-piece, ragged cotton prison uniform didn't keep out the cold. He shivered and reached his arms towards the burning wood to soak up the warmth.

Jared rolled a cigarette and handed it to Ramsey. He lit it and then rolled another for himself. Jared pulled up a chair and they sat there smoking side by side.

"Thanks, Jared," Ramsey said. He drew in heavily on the cigarette, enjoying it until the sheriff stomped over. He kicked Jared's chair.

"Git yer ass up," Noble growled.

Jared jumped up.

"What's the matter, Sheriff?"

"Thet's yer last warnin', bub! I ain't gonna tell ya again! Stay the hell away from the prisoner!"

"Whatever you say, Sheriff," Jared said. He returned to the bar. The sheriff followed behind.

Jared ate another pickled egg. "You got any beer, Ted?" he asked.

"Some local brews," Lowry replied.

Jared pointed. "That one, in the corner there."

"Satin's Left Nostril?"

"No, next to it."

"Rattlesnake Piss?" Lowry said, pointing to another bottle.

"Yeah, that's the one. Is it any good?"

"I know the old lady who makes it," Lowry said as he handed Jared the flip-top bottle. "She's crazy as a loon."

"Oh? What's in it?" Jared asked as he popped it open. Foam bubbled up over the top. Jared waited until it had stopped.

"Ah, you don't want to know, friend," Lowry chuckled. "But it ain't killed nobody yet, so it must be okay."

The sheriff scowled and said, "It smells like donkey piss ta me."

Jared eyed the bottle for a moment then took a sip. Lowry and the sheriff waited for his response.

Jared nodded. "Not bad. Tastes like potatoes and yeast. A little on the sweet side. But it has a little kick."

The sheriff chuckled. "Hell, if it's thet good, I'll have one, too."

Ted handed a bottle of Rattlesnake Piss to the sheriff. After it stopped foaming he took a pull, swallowed and nodded.

"Good piss," he said.

"Hey, Sheriff," Jared said. "How about I buy a beer and a couple of eggs and some jerky for the prisoner. Sort of as a last meal before the execution."

The sheriff gave that some thought. "Aw, hell, go ahead. It's yer money. But leave yer iron here."

"Sure, Sheriff."

Jared laid a double eagle and his gun on the bar. Lowry handed him a bottle of Rattlesnake Piss. Jared grabbed two eggs, a piece of jerky, and some hardtack and took it over to Ramsey.

"Merry Christmas," Jared chuckled.

"Much obliged, friend," Ramsey said. "I was just about to drop from hunger."

Ramsey went at the food in a frenzy. He finished and handed the bottle back to Jared.

"You're a real cowboy, Jared," Ramsey said. "I'll remember you in my will, friend."

Jared took the empty bottle back to the bar and went back to his unfinished beer. He picked up his gun.

Suddenly loud shouting came from the table where Weber, the deputy, and Val, the driver, were playing cards.

"You cheatin' bastard!" Weber yelled.

They both jumped up and drew. Val was a second faster and shot Weber in the heart. He went spinning and tumbling across the floor, knocking over some chairs.

"You dirty sonofabitch!" The sheriff bellowed. He drew and fired at Val. His bullet took the driver in the chest and sent him flipping over a table where he lay on his back looking up.

Jared and Lowry glanced at one another for a moment.

"Shit!" The barman walked slowly over to the scene and checked out both bodies. He looked back at the sheriff. "They're both dead."

Ramsey chuckled. "That's too bad."

"What the hell ya laughin' at, Ramsey!" Noble yelled. The veins stood out on his flushed face. "I ought ta plug yer ass, too!"

"Sure, go ahead, Sheriff," Ramsey said. "Explain that to Leavenworth!"

"I'll say ya tried ta escape. You killed Weber and Val, here, too, an' I shot ya. Thet's what I'll say!"

"You'll have to kill Jared here and the barman, too. I don't think they'll lie for you, asshole."

There was a moment of silence.

"What're we gonna do now, Sheriff?" Lowry asked.

"Shut up!"

The lawman was shaking. He looked around, suddenly realizing that he was outnumbered. Weber had been his shield and now he was dead.

"Don't anyone try anything funny," the sheriff said. "I'm still the law here." His voice broke when he spoke. "An' don't any of you forget it."

Lowry asked again, "But what are we gonna do, Sheriff?"

"I'm thinkin', damn it!" the sheriff exploded. He inhaled deeply and exhaled as he stared at the bodies. Finally, he pointed. "Take them two outside with the others. Make it quick!"

Jared looked at Ted Lowry. They nodded to each other then went to work. In half an hour, they had the job done. They came back brushing snow off their coats.

"Listen up," the sheriff said. "Anyone try anything funny an' I'll blow yer head off! I'm the law and don't one of you forget it!"

"Relax, Sheriff," Jared said. "Nobody is going to do anything funny."

"Both of you git over here. I don't want nobody close to the prisoner."

Jared walked over to the bar again. The sheriff watched him closely. "Thet's better."

Ramsey sat in his chair leaning close to the fire, smiling as if he had a surprise up his sleeve.

Lowry got a rag, a brush, and a pail of water from one of the rooms, got down on his hands and knees and started cleaning up the blood on the floor.

The wood in the fireplace was low. Ramsey tossed in some more wood from the wood box to get it higher. Jared went around straightening up the tables and chairs.

A half hour later, the place looked as if nothing had happened.

That's when they heard the sound out on the road. It was the sound of horses straining to pull a coach against the high snow. The sound got louder and louder until it stopped in front of the door.

"You expectin' any coaches?" Sheriff Noble asked.

"No," Lowry said. "Not until the morning."

The barman, the outlaw, the sheriff and the cowboy all stood staring at the door. The sound of the oncoming coach rose above the whistling of the wind.

Suddenly they heard the metallic sound of brake shoes grinding against iron. Horses whinnied and strained against the weight of the coach.

Finally, the stagecoach came to a complete stop in front of the door.

4.

The first to enter was a man fully dressed in black. His wide-brimmed hat and coat were dusted with snow as if he had been exposed to the elements. The hat hid most of his face, exposing only a thin, stern, down-curved mouth and a cleft chin. Stepping a few feet inside the door, the man opened his long coat to reveal two fully loaded gunbelts with twin Colts. His eyes carefully swept the room, taking everything in. He appeared to be about forty. He stood beside the open door, waiting.

After the man in black came another man, a short man, perhaps in his late fifties, wearing a fedora, gloves and a wool coat. His metal-rimmed spectacles were fogged over. He removed them to reveal dark, beady eyes set in a pale face. He had an air of authority about him as he cleaned his glasses with a white linen handkerchief and put them back on. Everything about him said wealth and confidence. He went immediately to the bar.

The last to enter and close the door was a woman seemingly in her early forties.

Atop her head was a gray, wide-brimmed felt hat that hid all but the tip of her delicate chin. She wore a mink coat, kidskin gloves, and delicate footwear. A long, flowing purple dress peeked out beneath her coat. She was without a doubt wealthy as well as attractive.

She removed her hat to reveal an abundance of auburn hair tied up in a bun. Her eyes were large and blue, and her mouth was full but somewhat pouting. She was very pretty, close to being beautiful.

Her eyes quickly fastened on the glowing fire and she walked swiftly towards it. Jace Ramsey moved aside to make room. Their eyes locked for a moment then she looked away into the flames. She held her gloved hands near the fire, a bit unsteady on her feet. The outlaw caught the smell of alcohol on her breath, along with the scent of her perfume.

Tired of being ignored, Sheriff Noble cleared his throat to get attention.

"I'm Sheriff Dan Noble," he said with loud authority. "Would someone tell me what's going on here? Where in the hell did you all come from? A party?"

The small man in the fedora and wool coat walked over to face the sheriff, staring at him sternly.

"My name is J.D. Dalgren, Sheriff," the man said in a patronizing voice. "I own this stage line, as well as the Dalgren Brewery in Kansas City and the Cattlemen's Savings and Loan in Perryville."

The sheriff suddenly realized who he was talking to.

"For God's sake, Mr. Dalgren, sir, what are you doing out on a horrible night like this?"

"I'm on my way to Kansas City. My mother is gravely ill there," Dalgren said. He pointed. "My wife and personal bodyguard are with me."

"Is that a carryall you're traveling in, Mr. Dalgren? It sounded like one."

"It's my private coach, why?"

"Well, it ain't gonna get you ta Kansas City in this kind of weather, sir. The snow is gettin' hip-deep out there."

"Yes, it caught us by surprise as we left Junction City," J. D. Dalgren said. He looked over at Ted Lowry. "Barman, where's the station attendant?"

"I'm the attendant, sir," Ted said.

"I'd like to send a telegram to Kansas City."

"Then you'll have to go on to the way station twenty miles up the line, Mr. Dalgren. We're just a swing station for changing horses."

J. D. Dalgren nodded. "Oh, yes. I forgot. What about the coach I saw as we came in? That would get us to Kansas City if we added all the horses to it."

"That coach is mine, sir," the sheriff said. "I'm afraid I can't let you have it."

"Oh? And why not?"

"Two reasons. First, my horses are just about run out, and second, I'm headed fer Leavenworth with that prisoner over there, Jace Ramsey."

Dalgren looked over to the fireplace where his wife stood talking to Ramsey.

"Darling!" he hollered, "come away from him. That's the man who robbed our bank in Perryville!"

When she didn't move, the sheriff shouted at the outlaw.

"Ramsey, go sit down!"

Ramsey nodded. He walked over to a table and sat down. Mrs. Dalgren gave the sheriff a cold look. J. D. Dalgren turned back to the sheriff.

"Would you divert to Kansas City on the way to Leavenworth, Sheriff?"

"I don't know about that, Mr. Dalgren. I'm on official law business. I'm sworn ta deliver the prisoner to Leavenworth."

"I could make it profitable for you, Sheriff," Dalgren said.

"You're not talking bribery, Mr. Dalgren, are you?"

"No, not at all, Sheriff. I'm only trying to appeal to your sense of humanity. Imagine if your mother was dying. What would you do?"

The sheriff gave that remark a moment's thought, then looked around the room to make sure no one could hear his reply.

"Let's go over here and talk about this, Mr. Dalgren," the sheriff whispered. He led the man to a corner out of earshot.

Mrs. Dalgren walked slowly over to Ramsey's table and sat down staring at him. She took a flask of whiskey from her coat pocket, took a drink, and then handed it to him. The outlaw took a long drink and gave it back.

"Thank you, ma'am."

"My name is Judith. Judith Dalgren. Are you really the man who robbed our bank in Perryville?" Her voice was heavy with drink and she slurred her words somewhat.

"Yes, ma'am."

"Your name is, what's your name?"

"Jace. Jace Ramsey, ma'am."

Judith Dalgren stared at the outlaw as if she was going to eat him for supper. "That's a beautiful name and you're a beautiful man."

Ramsey chuckled. "You're beautiful, too, Mrs. Dalgren. And that's a fact."

"Thank you. How come you're all handcuffed up like this, Jace Ramsey?"

"Well, ma'am, as you can see, I got caught."

"Caught where?"

"In a whorehouse in Belcher's Flats, a few months ago."

"Oh, I see."

"If I had known it was your bank in Perryville, ma'am, I wouldn't have robbed it. No sir. I sure wouldn't."

Judith Dalgren laughed scornfully. "As far as I'm concerned, you can rob all his businesses. I really don't give a damn, Mr. Ramsey."

"You sound bitter, ma'am."

"Do I?" Judith chuckled. "Well, perhaps I have good reason to be."

"That bruise on your cheek, ma'am? His?"

She put a finger to her left cheek, by her eye. "Yes. His."

"Where is he from?"

"The east coast. He's a big investor out here. He's got his fingers in a lot of pies."

"How long have you been married, if I'm not too nosey?"

"Twenty years."

"How was it?"

"Good for a while, until money took over. He pushed Paul, our son, over the edge. Paul couldn't stand it any longer and blew his own brains out, instead of his father's."

Suddenly she began to shiver. She sobbed quietly. Ramsey put his big, rough hand on her small-gloved one.

Suddenly the sheriff yelled across the room.

"Ramsey!"

The outlaw stood up and bowed to Mrs. Dalgren

"My pleasure, Mrs. Dalgren."

"And mine," she responded.

As Ramsey walked away, J.D. Dalgren rushed over and stopped him near the fireplace.

"You scum! How dare you put a hand on my wife?"

The sheriff came over and glared into Ramsey's face.

"What the hell did you do, Ramsey, assault Mrs. Dalgren, you sonofabitch?"

"Perhaps we should just hang him here and save the taxpayers a lot of money," J. D. Dalgren said. "Then you wouldn't have to go to Leavenworth, Sheriff."

The sheriff shrugged. "I'd have ta have a good reason ta do that, Mr. Dalgren."

"Well, he'll have to pay for assaulting my wife," the businessman said. He snapped the fingers of his right hand. "Come over here, Mr. Simms."

Judith Dalgren stood up. She looked terrified.

29

"Don't hurt him, J.D., please!"

Dalgren ignored his wife's plea. He smiled cruelly at Ramsey while repeating, "Mr. Simms! Come over here."

Simms, the man in black, walked quickly over to his boss. "What is it, Mr. Dalgren?"

"Simms," Dalgren said, "this man has insulted and touched Mrs. Dalgren. Teach him a lesson, please. One he will never forget. And if it, well, if it happens to prove fatal to him, I'm sure the sheriff won't mind at all."

Dalgren turned, took the sheriff's arm and led him over to the bar.

"Two whiskeys, barman," he said. The sheriff had an uncertain look on his face. He glanced back at Simms for a moment, then shrugged and looked away.

Simms took off his coat and hat, laid them on a chair then came back to face Ramsey. He cracked the knuckles of his big-boned hands, smiled and drove his right fist into the outlaw's stomach.

As Ramsey doubled over, Simms swung a vicious roundhouse left to the outlaw's right eye and then a right uppercut. Each blow connected and snapped Ramsey's headfirst sideways, then backwards. He dropped to his knees, groaning in pain as Simms hammered him with two more blows to the head, knocking him unconscious. The outlaw sighed and fell back flat.

J.D. Dalgren glanced over and raised his eyebrows in interest, nodding.

"Good work, Simms. Now stand him up."

Simms grabbed Ramsey by the hair and yanked him up into a kneeling position, then slapped his face until he came around. The outlaw finally gasped for air. He spit a mouthful of blood on the floor.

"On your feet, friend," Simms said calmly, without any sign of emotion. It was all in a day's work for him. "We ain't finished just yet."

Ramsey groaned and struggled to stand up. Blood ran down both sides of his face. His left cheek was split near his eye. He forced a smile and looked at Simms.

"Hell, is that all you got, baby girl?"

"I guess you want more, huh?" Simms pulled his right fist back. "Should I give him another dose of humility, sir?"

"No, no!" Dalgren said. "Hold on a moment."

The banker walked over to Ramsey and stared up into his eyes. "You don't look so well, Mr. Ramsey. Are you tired? Oh, well, hang on for a few more moments. It'll be all over soon and you can sleep as long as you want."

He turned to Simms.

"Mr. Simms, please give me one of your guns and a belt."

Simms hesitated for a moment then shrugged. He unbuckled his left gunbelt and handed it to Dalgren with the gun still in its holster. The banker removed the gun and tossed the belt at Ramsey's feet.

"Buckle up, Mr. Ramsey!" Dalgren chuckled.

He began removing shells from the Colt, letting them drop on the floor.

The big outlaw tried to bend down to get the gunbelt but almost fell sideways. He fought to regain his balance.

"I can't get it," he said through puffed, split lips.

"I'll help." Jared walked over, picked the gunbelt up, and handed it to Ramsey.

"Thanks, friend." The outlaw tried to buckle the belt on but couldn't. "How about shootin' the bastard for me while you're at it?"

"Make it worth my while and I might just do that."

Jared buckled the belt around the outlaw's waist.

"How much would it take?" Ramsey asked, adjusting the belt to the right feel.

"Fifty percent of the Perryville money," Jared said.

"Thirty?"

"Forty," Jared replied.

"Okay, friend, forty," Ramsey said.

"Let's shake on it."

As they shook hands, the sheriff came over and pushed Jared aside. He unlocked Ramsey's handcuffs.

"Move away, Jared. We don't need you here."

Jared didn't move far. He stood watching Dalgren hand the Colt to Ramsey.

"There's only one bullet somewhere in there, Mr. Ramsey. I've removed the other five. If you're lucky, it will be right where you need it. If not? Well, that's life, isn't it? You see, I do have a sense of humanity."

Suddenly Jared stepped in front of Ramsey.

"Jared!" the sheriff yelled, "What the hell are you up to now? Get yer ass outta there!"

"I'm just going to even the odds up, Sheriff, that's all."

"Hell, if you wanna get yerself killed, then go ahead. It ain't my concern."

For a moment, Simms looked pleased. He'd get to kill two instead of one.

"Why?" Simms asked Jared. His face had a blank look, as if frozen that way. He waited for Jared's answer.

"Because you're an egg-sucking, ass-kissing piece of crap," Jared said. "And your breath stinks."

Simms grinned. He had big white teeth and a wide mouth. "You're dead, cowboy!" he said, as if it were a fact.

Simms drew fast but didn't quite get his gun out of its holster when Jared crouched low and fanned off two quick shots. The first bullet took Simms in the heart, and the second in the forehead. Simms's eyes rolled up in his head and his legs folded beneath him. He was dead before he hit the floor.

"Good God Almighty!" the sheriff yelled.

There was a deep silence as Jared reloaded his Colt. He put it away, reached into his coat pocket and pulled out a key ring with two keys on it.

"Where'd you get them keys, Jared?" the sheriff hollered.

"Off Weber's body," Jared answered.

"Well, yer in deep trouble now, mister! I'll have to put you under arrest!"

Jared ignored the threat. He tossed the keys to Ramsey.

Dalgren stood shaking, his face pale. He looked very frightened. He went to his wife. She pushed him away, went to the outlaw, and kissed him.

"Judith, you slut!" Dalgren yelled. He began to shake harder.

The sheriff watched Jared cautiously as he walked to the bar. Lowry poured him a drink.

"It's on the house," Lowry said. "Christ, yer fast fer a cowboy. You just beat a professional gunslinger."

"I've gone up against faster ones than him," Jared said.

The sheriff suddenly looked scared and cornered.

5.

As the outlaw unlocked his leg shackles, Judith Dalgren picked up the five shells from the station floor. She took Ramsey's Colt and loaded it. He watched.

"You're pretty good, ma'am," he said.

"I've been around guns before," she answered. "We have a ranch near Hays City. I spend the summers there riding and hunting." She shoved the gun back in Ramsey's holster and pulled a handkerchief from her coat pocket. "Let me," she said and gently wiped the blood from Ramsey's bruised face.

She casually kissed his split lips, getting blood on her own. Her husband's face turned from pale white to purple rage. He cursed and rushed at her with a clenched fist raised to strike. Ramsey caught him by the wrist, slapped him hard across the face and shoved him away.

"Yer done hitting women," the outlaw said.

"Damn your soul, Judith," Dalgren cried. "You're finished! Finished, do you hear? You can go to hell for all I care but don't come home, ever!"

Dalgren was spitting mad. His body was trembling with uncontrollable rage. Saliva sprayed out of his mouth as he spewed words condemning his wife. Finally exhausted, he turned to the sheriff.

"Kill him, Sheriff," he said, pointing at Ramsey. "You have the right, now that he's armed! Do it and I'll make you a rich man!"

The sheriff stared at Dalgren for a moment then made a decision. Going for his gun, he snapped off a shot. It was meant for Ramsey but missed. It took Judith Dalgren's hat off.

Ramsey stepped left and fanned off a shot hitting the sheriff in the chest. The shock caused the lawman to trigger off a wild round. It hit J.D. Dalgren in the back of his head, killing him instantly. Both men fell lifeless to the floor.

Everyone froze in place for a moment, staring at the bodies of the sheriff and Dalgren, not saying anything. Finally, the barman spoke.

"Jesus!" Lowry muttered. "What the hell was that?"

Jared had an amazed look on his face. "I don't know. Maybe it was some weird kind of justice. I never saw anything like that before."

"She's hit!"

Ramsey was holding Judith Dalgren in his arms. Jared rushed over to help him get her to a chair while Lowry got the medicine box. The barman saw blood on her left temple. She had a wound but it wasn't deep. The bullet had cut a crease in the flesh along the side of her left cheek.

Lowry cleaned the wound and left it to dry.

"It ain't deep, ma'am, but it's gonna be sore for a while. It ain't bleeding."

"Thank you," Judith said. She looked pale. All the killing had gotten to her. There lay three dead bodies and one was her husband.

She began to cry and laugh at the same time. She looked around at Lowry, Ramsey and Jared, tears running down her face.

"Are you alright, ma'am?" Jared asked.

"I've never been better, Mr. Jared," she said. "I am now a very wealthy widow, thanks to Mr. Ramsey."

She began to laugh hysterically again, sobbing in between.

"Get her a drink," Ramsey said.

Lowry ran off to the bar and came back with a bottle of whiskey and a glass. He poured a drink and handed it to Mrs. Dalgren.

"You had best drink this, ma'am." The barman said. "It'll do ya good."

"Thank you," Judith said and emptied the shot glass in one pull, then shivered and chuckled. "It tickles all the way down, doesn't it?"

"Yes, ma'am," Lowry said, smiling. "You need another one?"

"No. That'll do for now. I'm fine."

"Sure," Lowry said and went back to the bar.

Jared pointed to Simm's body.

"He's about your size, Ramsey. You'd best get out of that prison uniform, don't you think?"

Ramsey went over to Simm's body and stood there measuring it with his eyes.

"Yeah, I was thinking the same thing," Ramsey said. He turned to Judith Dalgren. "Would you kindly turn yer head a moment, ma'am? I'll be getting naked."

"I've seem men before, Mr. Ramsey. Just pretend I'm not here. If you need help, let me know."

Jared walked over to the bar to talk to Lowry.

"Ramsey and me will be leaving at daylight. We'll need food for a week, at least."

"Sure," Lowry said, "I've got a larder full. Take yer pick. I'll make breakfast at sunrise."

"What are you gonna tell them about what happened here?"

"I don't rightly know. The truth, I guess. I couldn't lie better than this."

"Yeah, it's so crazy nobody will believe you anyway," Jared chuckled. "One thing, though."

"What's that?"

"I was never here."

The barman nodded. "Sure. Okay. You were never here. But I'm sure glad you were."

Jared chuckled.

Later they put Ramsey's prison uniform on Simm's body. Mrs. Dalgren took her husband's wallet and an envelope full of hundred-dollar bank notes and put them in her coat pocket.

Ramsey, Lowry and Jared dragged Simms, the sheriff and J.D. Dalgren outside behind the station with the other bodies. It was snowing as hard as before and getting much colder.

Back inside, they stoked up the fire again. Lowry got some blankets from the back room. One of the two rooms was a larder, and the other was where Lowry usually slept. But it was too cold back there and he preferred to nap before the fire.

The best they could do was to sit close together in chairs before the warm flames, wrapped in two blankets. The only one who managed to fall asleep was the outlaw, Jace Ramsey.

The rest were thinking about the horrible events of the evening.

6.

"You look very fine dressed in black, Mr. Ramsey," Judith Dalgren said. "It suits you well."

Ramsey smiled. He was wearing Simm's black hat, shirt, vest, pants, boots, and long coat. He did indeed look like a gunslinger.

Lowry had gone to great lengths to lay out a full breakfast of bacon, eggs, grits, and coffee on the plank bar.

"Come with me, Judith," Ramsey said after they had eaten.

"It would be bad for you if I did," she said. "They would say you kidnapped me. They'd hang you."

"It'd be too hard for her," Jared said. "She's not used to that kind of life, Ramsey."

Ramsey nodded. "Yeah. You're right, Jared. She wouldn't make it."

Lowry came from the back room with his coat on.

"I have to go up to the way station."

"How come?" Jared asked.

"I gotta tell them what happened here."

"Then take the sheriff's coach. You should take Mrs. Dalgren with you."

"Alright."

"Ramsey and I will come behind with a packhorse and one extra for you, in case we need it."

"I'd rather Mr. Ramsey and I ride in my carryall together," Mrs. Dalgren said. "He's still a bit under the weather after last night."

"Alright," Jared said. "If that's what you want, ma'am."

He didn't like that idea but kept quiet.

Later Lowry, Ramsey and Jared got the three outlaw horses that were tied in the pine trees behind the station and brought them around front. They stripped the gear off one and tied three saddlebags full of supplies on its back.

Jared's horse, already watered and fed, and was ready to go.

Lowry harnessed one of the big horses from the sheriff's coach to the carryall, and Mrs. Dalgren and Ramsey climbed in. Jared tied the two outlaw horses and the packhorse to the tailgate of the carryall.

Lowry got up in the driver's box, took up the reins, and looked down at Jared. Jared nodded, Lowry snapped the reins and they started out for the way station.

It had stopped snowing. The road ahead was buried under a six-inch layer of hard snow but the thin wheels of the carryall cut it like a knife. They made good time.

They were on the road no more than ten minutes when Mrs. Dalgren dropped the canvas curtains of the carryall. Jared saw this and it worried him. He hoped she wouldn't change her mind. It would complicate things badly.

It was mid-afternoon when they reached the way station. Lowry jumped down and waited for Mrs. Dalgren and Ramsey to get out of the carryall. When they did, instead of going into the way station, she followed the outlaw around behind it. He untied the horses and helped her up onto one. Once she was in the saddle, Ramsey then got on the other one and grabbed the reins of the packhorse.

Without a word, Mrs. Dalgren and the outlaw rode down the road with the packhorse tied to her saddle.

"Goodbye, Mr. Lowry!" she shouted.

Lowry stood by the carryall looking confused and lost. "Jesus!" he said, looking at Jared. "What the hell am I gonna tell them inside?"

Jared chuckled. "Oh, you'll think of something, kid." He rode off to catch up with the others.

Ten miles down the road, they came to a small town with a beanery and went in to eat. They talked over a hot bowl of chili.

"Where are we headed?" Jared asked.

"Cold Stone Gap," Ramsey said. "My boys will be at the hotel there." He chuckled. "They're gonna be mad as hell when they find out what you and Lowry did to my two men back at the swing station."

"They asked for it," Jared said.

Ramsey chuckled again. "Yeah. They didn't have half a brain between 'em." He looked across the table at Mrs. Dalgren. "Are you alright, Judith? Do you need anything?"

"No, Jace, I'm fine."

"When we get to Belcher's Flats, I'll see you get a decent room at the hotel there."

"How far is it?" Jared asked.

"We'll be there by sundown," Ramsey replied.

Soon they were back on the road. Just before dark they rode wearily into Cold Stone Gap.

Five miles off the old coach road was a small cattle town by the East Kansas River. It was a cowboy's town. When they came to raise hell on a Friday night, the marshal had sense enough to stay out of sight. He knew the storm would blow itself out by morning and all he had do was pick up the dead dogs and cats. The street would be deserted again and everything would be back to normal.

They left their horses at the stable at the east end of town and walked up the only street to the Blue Swan Saloon and Hotel, a three-story frame building painted blue.

As they walked through the foyer to the sign-in counter, all eyes were on Judith Dalgren.

The saloon was to the right and the dining room was to the left. A set of stairs, carpeted in red, led to the rooms.

"I'm afraid I'm out of ready cash," Ramsey said. A sign behind the counter demanded cash only.

"I've got it," Jared said. "How long?"

"Three days, at most," Ramsey replied.

"Three rooms for three days," Jared told the old man behind the counter.

"Make that two rooms," Ramsey corrected.

"Twelve dollars. Rooms 10 and 11. Upstairs." The man tossed Jared the keys.

Jared paid and they walked up the worn carpet to the second floor. Jared gave Judith Dalgren the key to room 11. She glanced at Ramsey as she went in.

"I'll see you down in the bar later," the outlaw said to Jared and went in behind Mrs. Dalgren.

Jared stood there a moment staring at the door then turned and went into room 10. He laid his saddlebag on a broken chair and looked around. It was a seedy room that smelled of cigarette smoke, urine and whiskey. He chuckled, wondering what Mrs. Dalgren would think of all this.

There was a nightstand with a water basin and pitcher of water in one corner. The water in the pitcher had a crust of ice on it. Jared broke it, poured water into the basin, and washed his hands and face. After that, he lay down on the smelly horsehair mattress.

An awful stink arose from beneath the mattress.

Jared got up, looked under the bed and saw the source of the odor. It was the chamber pot. He reached underneath, grabbed it by the handle and took it quickly to the window. Holding his nose, Jared tossed its contents outside onto the snow below then dropped it in a far corner of the room. After that, he lay down on the bed again.

He was worried about Judith Dalgren. She had let her emotions overcome her common sense and had no idea what she was getting into. As for Ramsey, he should have known better.

"I might have to kill him," Jared said softly to himself. "After I get the money."

Finally, he managed to doze off.

7.

When Jared woke up the room was dark and cold. The old cast-iron bed creaked as he sat up on the edge of it. He waited a while until his head cleared and then went down the stairs to the foyer. He stood there looking into the bar. It was packed.

A mixed crowd of cowboys and townsfolk milled about in a sea of bodies, talking, laughing, and shouting. Somewhere behind it all, someone was playing a violin that was about fifty degrees out of tune. Couples danced on top of sawdust in a small, cleared area.

Jared made his way past the tables and groups of babbling cowboys until he came to the bar. Once there he ordered a local beer to moisten his dry mouth. It tasted bitter but it was wet and that's all that mattered.

He looked around and saw Ramsey and Judith Dalgren swaying in close embrace in the middle of the dance floor. She seemed deep in thought as they moved slowly in smooth circles to the rhythm of the waltz.

From time to time she looked up, kissed him and put her head on his shoulder, smiling. They both seemed happy. Suddenly Jared felt sorry for her. This would never last. She was living an illusion and working hard at it.

When the dance ended, they walked over to Jared.

"Come on an' meet the boys," Ramsey said.

Judith avoided looking at him as they walked over to a far table by the wall where four of Ramsey's outlaws sat drinking and playing cards. When they saw Ramsey, Jared and Mrs. Dalgren, they put the cards down.

"Men," Ramsey said, "this is the hombre I told you about, the one who saved my ass fair and square." He patted Jared on the back. "Jared, these are Ernie, Lester, Phil and Sammy. All damn good men."

Jared nodded as each name was said.

There was an open space with two empty chairs. Ramsey pulled one out for Judith. She sat down. He sat beside her.

"Pull up a chair," Ramsey told Jared.

Jared found an empty chair by the wall and forced his way in beside Mrs. Dalgren and Ernie. Ernie didn't seem to like that so much. He gave Jared a severe look.

"Jared is a loner, boys," Ramsey went on, "and he's fast with a gun. I figure we could use him since Red and Al are frozen stiff back at that swing station. Whatta think about that, Ernie?"

Ernie gave Jared a sour look that didn't make him feel very welcome.

"Yer the boss, Jace," Ernie muttered, shrugging. He gave the others a knowing look. It was a code.

Jace Ramsey also saw the look and felt the tension. He smiled and laughed nervously. "Hell, let's all tie one on!"

"Yeah, let's do thet! Get pissy-faced drunk," one of the other outlaws, Phil, said.

"You said it, Phil," the one called Lester replied. "How about you, Sam?"

The one named Sam grinned and nodded. "Let's git it on!"

Sammy left and came back with two bottles of whiskey and some extra glasses. Jared nursed his beer while the others drank.

Ernie asked Mrs. Dalgren for a dance. She hesitated, looking at Ramsey for help.

"Go ahead, Judith," Ramsey said.

Judith got up and followed the outlaw into the crowd. They were gone only a few minutes when Sammy, Lester and Phil got up and walked over to join them, taking turns dancing with Judith.

Jared was concerned. "They're ganging up on her, aren't they, Ramsey?"

"She's fine," Ramsey said. "I've got them on a short rope. They'll behave themselves."

Jared took a sip of his beer. "What about the money?"

"What money?"

"The seventy-five thousand from the Perryville job. My forty percent?"

"Oh, that," the outlaw said. "Well, it's tucked away at Wamego Falls."

"Where the hell is Wamego Falls?"

Ramsey laughed. "What, you don't know?"

"I asked, didn't I?"

"Yeah, you did."

"So, where is it?"

"North of Junction City, above the Kansas River."

"Never heard of it."

"Not many have. That's why I chose it ta stash the money away," Ramsey said.

"When are we leaving?" Jared asked, trying to sound casual. Ramsey knew different.

"Soon. In a couple of days."

After that, they didn't say anything significant.

Judith came back alone from the dance floor. Her hair and dress were in disarray and she was flushed. She gave Jared a glance as she sat down.

The four outlaws emerged from the crowd and came up to the table laughing.

"Come on, Judy," Ernie said. "We're jest gettin' started, baby! I ain't even warmed up yet!

The outlaw reached for Judith's arm but Jared brushed it away.

"The lady is tired, boys. She's had a long, rough day."

"No, she ain't," Ernie said. "She ain't done 'til I say she's done. Right, Jace?"

For a moment Jace Ramsey looked uncertain, then conflicted. He blurted out, "Whatever you say, Ernie."

As the outlaw reached for Judith Dalgren again, Jared stood up and stepped between them.

"I believe this one is mine, Ernie," Jared said.

Jared and the outlaw glared at one another, sizing each other up.

"Hell, Ernie," Ramsey said. "Let him have this one."

Ernie dropped his hand down by his gun and for a moment, it looked like he was going to draw. Jared dropped his hand down, too, and stared at the outlaw with a calm, cold, unblinking eye, looking right into the outlaw's soul.

"It's your call, friend," Jared said smoothly, with a hard sneer on his lips. His voice had steel in it.

"Maybe some other time," the outlaw said. He sat down and poured himself a drink.

Jared took Judith gently by the hand and she followed him out onto the dance floor. She came into his arms and they danced.

"Thank you, Clay," she said.

When the dance was finished, Jared led her out into the foyer.

"Go up to your room, ma'am," Jared said. "I'll tell them you don't feel well."

Judith nodded and went up to her room. Jared went back to join the outlaws. When they saw he was alone, they stared hard at him.

"Where is she?" Phil asked.

"She isn't feeling well," Jared replied.

Phil chuckled. "Yer a slick one, ain't ya, Jared?"

"No, Phil," Jared said, staring hard at the outlaw. "What I am is a cowboy. Are you a cowboy, Phil?"

For a moment Phil looked sober. He was older than the other outlaws were.

"I was, once," Phil muttered.

"Then you know the code, I suspect," Jared said.

"Hell, let's change the subject," Ramsey chuckled. "We're getting too serious. Let's drink and swap tall stories. We were all cowboys, once."

"Hell, yeah!" Sammy said.

Jared switched from beer to rotgut. He got two more bottles and they sat at the table and did some serious drinking. Soon they were swapping tall stories and singing old songs. Some girls came over and they danced again into the early morning hours.

Jared got very drunk and slept late. When he woke up, he was seeing double and his head throbbed as if a bull had sat on it. He drank the ice cold water from the pitcher and poured some over his head to wake up.

When he finally did, he knew something was wrong. His gunbelt was missing and everything was too quiet. He dressed as fast as he could, went out and knocked on Judith Dalgren's door. When he got no answer, he tried the door handle and found it wasn't locked. He went in and saw the room was empty.

Jared checked the other outlaws' rooms and found them empty too. He went back to his room, got his coat and then ran stumbling down the stairs, trying not to fall. After looking into the dining room and not seeing them there, he rushed across town to the stable. His horse was gone and so were the others.

"They left early," the stable owner said. "They sure were in a hurry."

"Was the woman with them?"

"Yep. She sure is a looker, ain't she?"

"Yeah," Jared replied. "She sure is. They took my horse."

"Sorry ta hear thet."

Jared said, "If it gets a chance, it'll come back."

"Then I'll keep an eye out fer it," the man said. "I'll let ya know. Where ya bunkin'?"

"Room 10, at the Blue Swan."

It started to turn colder. Jared sighed and went back to the hotel.

8.

They made good time. By noon, Cold Stone Gap was thirty miles behind. Judith Dalgren was beginning to tire. She glanced over at Ramsey.

"Jace, I have to rest," she pleaded.

"We will, soon, Judith. Hang on a little longer. Just a few more miles."

It seemed more than that when they finally rode into a stand of pine trees near a stream. She was about to drop. Ramsey quickly dismounted and helped her down from her horse.

"I'm freezing," Judith whispered. She started to shiver.

Ramsey put an arm around her. "We'll build a fire."

In half an hour, they were standing around a mound of blazing pine needles and twigs. Judith pulled the collar of her fur coat up around her ears. She had lost her hat but couldn't remember exactly where. The wind had taken it sailing away miles back.

The outlaws passed around a bottle of whiskey.

"No," Judith said, when her turn came. "It makes me sick."

"Just take a nip," Ramsey said. "It'll warm you up."

She gave in, took a quick pull, made a sour face and shivered as it went down. The outlaws laughed. Judith handed the bottle to Sammy.

"Good girl," Ramsey chuckled.

Suddenly they heard a whinny and Jared's horse broke loose and ran into the woods.

"Kill it," Ernie shouted.

Phil drew and fanned off three shots at the fleeing animal.

"I think I hit it," he said.

"I hope you did," Ramsey said. "For your sake."

Half an hour later, they put the fire out and mounted up again. Judith had trouble.

"It's my legs. I can't," she said.

Ramsey lifted her up into the saddle.

"How far?" she asked.

"Not far," Ramsey said.

Not far turned out to be pretty far. It was sundown, four hours later, when they rode across the Kansas Pacific Railroad into Belcher's Flats, a collection of sod homes and wooden shacks in the middle of nowhere.

They tied their horses up at the largest building in town, a white clapboard house with an upper floor. It had a crude sign above the door that read: Dotty's Place. Ramsey led the way in.

It had a small central lobby with a barroom to the left and a beanery to the right.

A large-bosomed woman dressed in a red flannel shirt, woolen trousers held up by suspenders, and cowboy boots came around the registration counter and ran to Jace Ramsey. She threw her arms around his neck and kissed him full on the mouth.

"Jace Ramsey!" she yelled. "You sly fox, you! The last I heard you were being hung at Leavenworth!"

"Not yet, Dotty," Ramsey chuckled. "I'm still kicking up a storm, little darlin'."

Dotty noticed Judith Dalgren.

"Who's thet, lover boy? I thought I was yer only gal!"

"Dotty, this is Judith Dalgren."

The big woman grabbed Judith's hand and shook it.

"Welcome ta Dotty's Place, Judy," Dotty chuckled.

When the introductions were over Ramsey signed for what Dotty called the bridal room. It was a small, stuffy room with a large, king-sized brass bed with broken springs and a lumpy, horsehair mattress. It had the luxury of two chamber pots instead of one.

Ernie and Lester took the room to the left, and Phil and Sammy took the room to the right of Ramsey's room.

As they went into the bridal room, Judith Dalgren stopped Ramsey at the door.

"Jace, darling," she said with a deep sigh. "I'm very tired. Would you mind staying with the boys?"

Ramsey's face clouded over. For a moment, he looked angry. He quickly checked that and forced a smile. This wasn't what he had expected. Far from it. He knew the boys were listening.

"Alright, Judith, sure," Ramsey said.

"Thanks for being so understanding, Jace."

She kissed him lightly on the cheek and closed the door. He stood there a moment staring, then went next door into the room with Phil and Sammy.

"Is the honeymoon over, Jace?" Phil chuckled.

"She's got a headache," Ramsey said.

Sammy handed him the bottle of whiskey they had just opened. He took a swig.

"Say," Phil said. "Is she any kin of thet J. D. Dalgren, thet rich carpetbagger from Kansas City, whose bank we robbed?"

"Yep," Ramsey said.

"What the hell is she a-doin' hangin' out with you, Jace?" Sammy asked.

"It's a long story," Ramsey replied.

"Hell, let's hear it," Phil said.

"Okay."

When Ramsey was finished telling the story, Phil whistled and Sammy chuckled.

"I bet you kin get a hundred thousand for her if ya wanted to, Jace," Phil said. "Even more. Easy."

"Maybe," Ramsey said. "The thought has crossed my mind."

"How does thet work?" Sammy asked.

"You send somebody a message," Phil said, "and ask for money for her return."

"Is it thet easy?" Sammy asked.

"Sure," Phil, the expert, said. "Easy as pie. I could ride in ta Fort Riley and send a wire."

"Send a wire ta who?" Sammy asked.

"To the ol' man's headquarters in Kansas City. He has a big law office there."

Ramsey chuckled.

"You assholes! You don't know what the hell you're talking about. Even if you did get the money they would came after you. You'd be on the run for five, ten, twenty years. They would hire bounty hunters an' detectives. They would put a big reward on your heads. Even if they got the money back, they'd still come after you. They would never give up."

There was a heavy silence after that.

"What about Mexico?" Sammy asked.

"What about it?" Ramsey replied.

"They can't touch you in Mexico, can they?"

Ramsey shrugged and took a pull on the whiskey bottle.

"Maybe, maybe not. But the Mexicans would give you up for a gold double eagle and not even blink."

Phil sniffed, wiped his nose on his shirtsleeve and grabbed the bottle. "Hell, I heard ya kin bribe them Mexicans fer a few pesos."

"I'll tell ya what, Jace," Sammy said. "Why don't ya jest hand the lady over to us and you keep the seventy-five thousand from the Perryville heist?"

Ramsey suddenly felt conflicted. He hadn't expected things to turn in this direction. Just by bringing her here, he had put Judith Dalgren into danger's way. What was he thinking? He knew from the start she was way out of his class. She could never be an outlaw's woman. Maybe ransoming her off was the quickest and best way to get her to safety. If they thought she was valuable, they wouldn't harm her.

But not yet, not this soon. He wanted to spend more time with her. She had gotten under his skin and it would be hard to let this beautiful little bird fly free.

"Wait until we get to Wamego," Ramsey said. "We'll have more time to talk it over there."

"Sure," Sammy said. He gave Phil a look. Ramsey noticed.

"Yeah, boss," Phil said. He looked back at Sammy.

Ramsey suddenly realized they were thinking on their own and he didn't like it. They'd start questioning his decisions. That was the start of trouble. That's how gang leaders got shot in the back. For the first time Jace Ramsey noticed signs of rebellion in his gang and he felt a little uneasy.

In the next room, Judith Dalgren had her ear against the wall. She heard every word spoken. She had a worried look on her face.

Reality began to quickly set in.

9.

A day after Jared was left stranded in Cold Stone Gap, a boy found him in the bar of the Blue Swan Saloon.

"Yer horse is back, mister," the boy said. Jared gave him a penny and went down to the stable. His horse was in a stall eating a bag of oats. Jared looked him over.

"He got nicked in the right flank," the stableman said. "I put some salve on it. It ain't much' ta worry about."

Jared gave the horse a hug around the neck and rubbed its ears. He stayed with it until it had finished eating and drinking then gave the stableman four double eagles.

"Keep an eye on him," Jared said. "I'll be right back."

He walked up to the Blue Swan and went into the dining room and had breakfast, then went up to his room. He sat on his bed, thinking.

With a woman in a dress along, Ramsey and his men wouldn't be making fast time, and the snow was deep enough to hold them down to a fast walk. They'd make maybe twenty miles the first day.

As Jared lit a cigarette, he wondered why he was worried about Judith Dalgren. She had made her own choice. It wasn't his problem that she was in over her head. At some point, though, she was going to need help.

However, there was the money. Seventy-five thousand was sitting somewhere up in Wamego Falls. That was something to think about. His own money, four month's pay, was getting low. He'd have to find a job soon.

Jared got his saddle, saddlebag and Winchester out from under the bed then carried them down to the stable. He saddled up and rode north, remembering that Ramsey had mentioned that Wamego Falls was north of Belcher's Flat, above the Kansas River. They would be leaving a trail in the snow all the way.

The stableman showed Jared where Ramsey and his gang had ridden out from behind the stable. The trail the horses made in the snow was easy to follow. The six riders and a packhorse left a clearly cut path.

The trail left Cold Stone Gap, went northeast for several miles, then veered straight north into open country. After about fifteen miles, Jared found where they had stopped to build a fire. The woman was slowing them down. By late evening, Jared had followed the trail into Belcher's Flats. He tied up at the big, two-story building called Dotty's Place and went inside.

There were two men in the lobby and they stared at him as he entered. Jared dropped his hand down by his side to feel for his Colt but realized it was gone. They had taken his gunbelt. For a moment the men sized him up then looked away. It was as if they were expecting him.

Big Dotty greeted him in an affectionate way, giving him a hug and a kiss. Her breath was sour from whiskey. The way she acted, rotgut was her food of choice. Her eyes glowed. It was almost as if she were waiting for him, too.

"Howdy, handsome! Welcome ta Dotty's Place," Dotty said boisterously. "I own this dump! Hell, I own half the damn town." She laughed, exposing rotting teeth. "What's yer name, stranger?"

"Jared. Clay Jared."

Jared saw a flicker in the woman's eyes. That flicker told him plenty.

"What brings you this far north, cowboy?"

"I was supposed to meet some pals here but I guess I'm too early."

Dotty chuckled. "Ya might be too late, friend, if yer talkin' about who I think you are."

"Jace Ramsey?"

"Yep! Him an' his pals left a day ago. Headed north fer Wamego."

"Darn it! Well, I guess I'd best get back in the saddle then."

The big woman put a hand on Jared's arm and pouted.

"Hey! Relax, cowboy," she said seductively. "There's no rush, is they? Let 'em go. Hell, you kin go up there tomorrow. Let 'em freeze their asses off."

"What's up there?" Jared asked casually.

"There ain't a damn thing up there. Jest an old deserted mining camp, wolves and bears," Dotty said. Suddenly, a cloud fell over her face. "The place is haunted."

"Haunted?" Jared laughed.

"Ya kin laugh if ya want to, cowboy, but it's a fact." Dotty screwed her face up. Her eyes narrowed as she glared at a vision. "They started killin' each other over the gold. They found jest one alive, and he was shot, half dead an' crazy as a loon."

Jared decided to play along. "Sounds scary. Maybe I'd better not go up there."

"Now yer talkin' sense, cowboy," Dotty said. "I bet yer thirsty and tired. I'll give ya a room an' send up a bottle and a nice lookin' girl. It's on the house."

"Now that sounds like a good deal," Jared laughed. "But how come?"

"How come? Hell, any pal of Jace Ramsey is a pal of Dotty's. That's how come. Jace Ramsey is fair an' square in my book!"

Dotty got a key to room 9 and handed it to Jared.

"Thanks, ma'am," Jared said. He pointed toward the bar, to the right. "I'll grab a couple of eggs and some jerky first, if you don't mind."

"You go ahead. I'll send thet little package up to yer room. It'll be a-waitin' fer ya."

"I'll look forward to it," Jared chuckled, smiling big.

73

Jared stood at the bar with a bottle of homemade beer and wolfed down three eggs and a piece hardtack. He couldn't see the two men but he knew they were near, watching him. He was sure Ramsey or his men had set it up. They wanted him dead. Ramsey had never intended to split the money with him.

Dotty didn't ask him why he was going up to Wamego Falls but Jared figured she knew Ramsey was going there to get the seventy-five thousand dollars. Then he would come back to Belcher's Flats. It would make a good place for Ramsey to hide out. Dotty would shield him from the law. For a price, of course.

She practically owned the town. Ramsey would count on that. The law would never find him here, and, if they came, he could go back up to Wamego Falls. Nobody would get him there.

Now those two men would kill Jared for a piece of the pie. With seventy-five thousand dollars, Ramsey could buy the whole town.

Jared suddenly realized that, since he had no weapon, there was no way he could get out of the place alive. If he tried to run for the door, they would gun him down in the street and stuff his body in an alley. If he went to the room, which is where Dotty wanted him to go, they would probably kill him in his sleep and toss his body out the window.

Either way he was a dead man.

After a few moments reflecting on his situation, Jared decided he would see what his options were. He walked into the lobby. One of the men stood by the front entrance smoking. Jared nodded to him and turned around, looking for the rear door. It was back between the stairway and the wall by the bar. Jared had started towards it when the second man came out of the shadows and stood next to it. He smiled at Jared.

Knowing now that both doors were covered, Jared walked towards the stairs and started up them to the room. The two men were right behind him. At the top landing, he stopped and turned to look at them.

"Hi, fellahs," Jared said.

"Keep going, smart ass," the tall one said, his hand down by his gun. His eyes were empty of emotion.

Jared shrugged, turned around and started walking again. When he got to room nine he unlocked the door and went in.

The two gunnies came in and watched as he went to the washstand and lit the oil lamp.

"She promised me a bottle of whiskey and a girl," Jared said to break the ice.

"She says thet to all of 'em," the short killer said.

"You guys do this often?"

"Often enough," the tall killer said.

Jared nodded. "Real tough guys, huh?"

"Yer gonna find out in one second, friend," the tall killer said.

"It's against the code to shoot an unarmed man," Jared said suddenly. "Only a yellow-belly coward would do a thing like that."

"Who you callin' yellah, cowboy?" the tall killer asked.

"You, you sonofabitch. You're a yellow-belly coward," Jared said with a smile. "You wouldn't make a pimple on a cowboy's ass. Yer mother should have drowned you at birth, you piece of crap!"

For a moment the tall killer was taken aback. He glared at Jared, his eyes bulging as he decided how to counter

Jared's accusations. Without taking his eyes off Jared, he spoke aside to his companion.

"Give the sonofabitch yer gun, Ike."

"What?"

The tall killer growled, "I said, give tha bastard yer gun!"

"Give him my gun?"

"You heard me, an' do it quick!"

"What the hell for, Rick?"

"I'm gonna kill him fair and square, that's what the hell for," the tall killer hissed.

For a moment Ike stared at Rick. Finally, he shrugged. "Okay, if thet's how ya want it." He unbuckled his gunbelt and tossed it to Jared.

Jared caught it. He turned his back to them as he buckled the gunbelt on.

"You gonna shoot me in the back?" Jared taunted.

"Nope," Rick said. "Yer gonna see it comin, you sonofabitch."

Jared held his hand out away from the holster and turned slowly around.

"How about we let your short pal make the call?" Jared said, smiling. "On three, if he can count that high."

That insult hurt Ike. "Kill the bastard, Rick!"

Rick drew. His gun was up and out but much too late as two of Jared's bullets smashed into his body.

They both hit him in the heart. He grunted and went flying straight back, slamming hard against the door. His body folded and he slid down into a sitting position with a blank look on his face.

"Jesus!" Ike whispered. He stared at Rick for a moment and then at Jared. His legs began to shake.

Jared reloaded the gun. "Nice gun. Mind if I keep it?"

"No, no!" Ike said. He sounded as if his mouth was dry.

"Thanks," Jared chuckled. He holstered the gun, went to the door, picked up Rick's gun and pushed his body aside. "If you make a sound I'll come back and shoot you in the balls. Understand?"

"Yes," Ike's teeth were chattering.

"Whose idea was it? Ramsey's?"

"No," Ike said. "It was Ernie. He made the deal with Dotty. She hired us an' promised us five hundred apiece."

"Ernie? What's he up to?"

"He's gonna kill Ramsey and take the money and the girl," Ike said. "Better fer her she kills herself. Ernie goes crazy around girls."

"Thanks for being honest," Jared said.

He went quickly out into the hall, locked the door to room and hurried down the stairs. He ran into Dotty.

"You!" was all she could manage to say.

"Yep, it's me," Jared said, stopping.

Just as she started to scream, Jared swung Rick's gun hard against the side of her head. Her eyes rolled up and she dropped slowly to the lobby floor in a heap.

Someone saw him and shouted. Jared ran outside across the porch and vaulted into the saddle.

As he rode across town he tossed Rick's gun into an alley. He looked back to see some men on the porch. One fired a shot at him but missed.

He kept riding.

10.

It was late afternoon when a coyote announced the arrival of six humans as they rode into the old, deserted mining camp at Wamego Falls. Crows looked down from their high perches in the nearby pines, cocked their heads and chattered. Snowflakes fell silently, dancing on the currents.

The metallic sound of horses' hooves rang loudly on the rocks and echoed through the cold emptiness of a place abandoned long ago.

"This is it, boys," Ramsey said.

"So, is this where ya was hidin' out all thet time we was leadin' the posse on a wild goose chase?"

"Yep! And it was a good plan," Ramsey said. "You guys dodged the posse and I got to hide the seventy-five-thousand. And now here we are. It all worked out. We'll split the money and head for Mexico. I'd say it all worked out fine."

"Yeah, mostly fer you," Phil said sarcastically. "Thet posse ran our asses ragged. We almost got caught."

"Yeah," Ernie chuckled, "an' you were in Belcher's Flats doin' the hoochy-coochy with one a Dotty's girls"

"An' got caught by the sheriff, too!" Lester chuckled.

The outlaw chief realized that he didn't look too smart in the eyes of his men anymore. While he was in jail the money was out of their reach and it shouldn't have been. If he had been hung in Leavenworth, it would have rotted away in this remote wilderness.

Ramsey looked away for a moment then gave Ernie a scowling stare. He didn't like being criticized. Ernie was getting too smart lately. He'd have to put him in his place. Maybe even kill him.

Judith remained on her horse as the men dismounted. They stood for a moment looking around, listening to the chorus of wolves singing to the fading sun.

There were several broken-down miner's shacks just inside the tree line in the open hardpan area. Across from them was a small stream that ran quietly over a bed of talus. A large, broken sluice box squatted by the stream, and rusted shovels and broken wheelbarrows lay discarded about. They could almost feel the ghosts of the long-dead miners walking around the place.

The miner's camp was surrounded by low mountains forming a protective bowl. An opening between them let the cold winter wind swoop screaming down from above. It cut across the line of trees into the bowl, making a whistling sound among the abandoned shacks.

Judith Dalgren was exhausted and chilled to the bone. She sat slumped in her saddle, unable to summon enough strength to dismount. Ramsey walked over to her and lifted her down. She leaned against the horse, clinging to the saddle horn.

"I need help, Jace," she said in a whisper. The wind whipped her hair loosely about her head.

Ramsey picked her up in his arms and carried her to the one shack with a roof and walls. The door was twisted on its rusted hinges. He kicked it aside and went in. In the gloom he made out a table and several wooden chairs. He set her down on the best one. It held. Ramsey looked around and chuckled.

"Yeah. This is the one," he muttered to himself.

"What?"

"Nothing," he replied. "I'll go and help build a fire."

"Don't leave me," she pleaded.

"I'll bring you hot coffee and jerky," he replied and left.

Judith pulled her fur coat up high and folded her arms to ward off the biting cold. Her mind raced. Clay Jared would be dead by now. She knew they'd set a trap to murder him. And here she was at the mercy of outlaws. It now was clear what a foolish, emotional woman she had been. Even a life with her horrible husband seemed more attractive at this point. If he were still alive, she would gladly go back to him on her knees and beg for forgiveness.

She sat listening as they built a fire out in front of the shack. There was talking and then arguing. Soon anger rose in the voices.

"You gonna let her have the best shack while we sleep out here on the ground, Jace?" Phil complained. "Thet ain't right!"

They had gotten the fire going and were standing around it, looking sullen.

"You taking over, Phil?" Ramsey asked coolly with a smile. "It sounds to me like you are, Phil."

Phil looked down into the fire and shifted his weight.

"I didn't say I was," Phil answered. "But maybe somebody ought to. You ain't treatin' yer own men right since you took up with her."

"Yeah, boss," Lester joined in. "You changed since ya been ta jail. You ain't like you was before ya met her."

"She's turned yer head, boss," Sammy said.

Ernie watched quietly, smiling as the argument got hotter. He seemed to be enjoying Ramsey's bad predicament.

"Jest give me my share of the money," Phil said, "an' I'll cut outta here. I ain't ridin' under you anymore, Ramsey!"

"I don't like that tone, Phil," Ramsey said. "I don't like it at all."

"Like it or not, I want my cut an' I ain't waitin' fer it," Phil growled.

"Yeah, me too, boss," Sammy said. "I'm headin' fer Mexico where the damn sun is a-shinin'. Ta hell with this place."

Ramsey looked across the fire at his men, suddenly aware that he was facing a mutiny. They'd have to kill him.

He knew it and they knew it. That's how it was. There was no honor among thieves, no mercy between killers.

Ramsey smiled and chuckled.

"Okay, men," he said cheerfully. "Relax. Phil and I will go get the money and bring it out. Okay, Phil?"

"Where is it?" Sammy asked.

"In the shack, where she is," Ramsey replied.

"You go ahead an' get it," Phil said. "I'll wait here with the boys, if it's all the same ta you."

Ramsey nodded. "Sure, Phil, whatever you say."

The outlaw chief turned away from the fire and walked slowly towards the shack, listening for any sounds behind him that might signal danger. He heard nothing. No, they wouldn't try to kill him before he showed them the money. He finally disappeared into the shack.

He went over and stood by Judith.

"Whatever happens, Judith, stay here," he said. "When it's over, I'll take you home."

Ramsey walked across the floor of rotting boards and stopped by a certain one. He got down on his knees, brushed away the accumulated dust and saw the big X he had carved into the wood. He took out his boot knife and pried it up far enough to reach under.

After fumbling for a few moments he pulled out a saddlebag. Each side was stuffed full with something.

"Is that the seventy-five-thousand dollars from my husband's bank, Jace?"

"Yes, Judith."

"It's no good to us, is it? They're going to kill us, aren't they?"

"Maybe it will save our lives, Judith. It's worth a try."

Ramsey stood up with the saddlebag and sighed. He turned to Judith.

"I'm sorry I got you into this, Judith," he said. "I never should have talked you into it."

Judith smiled. "I know, Jace. I know."

Ramsey walked over, bent down and kissed her.

"You're a real woman," he said.

"And you're a real cowboy," she replied. "Thank you for the wild ride. I'll never forget you."

Ramsey slung the saddlebag over his shoulder and walked outside.

Judith began to sob.

As Ramsey went through the door he saw they were lined up with their guns drawn. He walked over to the fire and chuckled.

"What's this, boys? You gonna bushwhack me?"

"Something like thet," Phil said. "We figure a four-way split is best."

"Is that right? All of you think that?"

They nodded.

"How about you, Ernie? You in on it, too?"

"Hell, yes, Jace," Ernie said. "It was my idea!"

Ramsey nodded, forcing a smile.

"I see," he chuckled. "Okay, then, here's yer money."

The outlaw tossed the saddlebag into the fire and drew. His shot hit Phil in the chest, but Ramsey was instantly knocked down by a dozen bullets from Ernie, Lester and Sammy who fanned off shot after shot until he lay dead on the ground.

Ernie kicked the saddlebag out of the flames. Lester bent down and checked Phil.

"He's bought the farm," Lester said. "Too bad."

"It's all thet bitch's fault!" Ernie growled.

"Yeah," Sammy said, "she needs ta be taken, an' taken good. Really good." He wiped his nose with the back of his hand and dried it on his shirt. "She needs ta be taken hard, is what needs ta happen ta her."

"I'll take her first," Ernie said.

"No! It was my idea ta take her, not yers!" Sammy said defensively. "Who the hell made you the boss?"

Ernie dropped his hand down by his gun and turned to face Sammy.

"If you wanna find out who's boss, go ahead and pull, pal," Ernie growled.

Lester cleared his throat. "Wait a minute, Ernie, it was Sammy's idea. It's only fair he gits ta go first, ain't it?"

For a moment Ernie looked undecided. Suddenly he smiled and said, "Hell, go ahead, if yer gonna cry about it, asshole. Go first, if ya want to."

Without waiting, Sammy puffed out his chest like a rooster and walked up to the shack. He stood there hesitating, looking back at the others. Finally, he grinned, nodded and stepped confidently through the doorway.

A second later, there was a popping noise.

"What the hell was thet?" Ernie asked.

"Hell, I don't know!" Lester replied.

Sammy appeared in the doorway holding a hand over his heart. He looked confused. His face was white as the snow.

"What the hell happened, Sammy?" Lester shouted.

"Shit! She had a peashooter," Sammy gasped. His legs were unsteady as he held onto the doorjamb for support.

"A peashooter?" Ernie asked.

"Yeah, a one-shot, forty-one caliber peashooter," Sammy gasped. He took three steps, then sat down in the snow. "She done kilt me, boys." Sammy toppled sideways with a heavy sigh and lay still, staring blankly over at the fire.

Lester screamed, "Thet dirty bitch! I'm a-gonna kill her!"

"Wait 'til I'm finished takin' her first," Ernie said. "Then I'll kill her."

"I ain't a-waitin' fer you ta get yer enjoyment outta her while poor ol' Sammy's a-layin' there dead as a mackerel." Lester screamed. "I'll kill you first!"

Lester drew on Ernie from ten feet away.

Ernie was too fast for Lester. He shot him in the stomach once, then in the heart and then in the head for good measure. Lester's body jerked with each shot. It spun and danced and then hit the ground with a thudding sound.

Ernie looked down at his once partner and chuckled.

"I guess it's all mine now," he chuckled. "The money and the girl."

He holstered his gun and looked up at the shack with a wide grin on his face. He went confidently to the packhorse and got a bottle of whiskey from the saddlebag.

"Hey, Mrs. Dalgren! Let's you an' me have a party!" Ernie hollered as he took a long drink from the bottle. He laughed. "Hot dog, this is gonna be so good!"

The outlaw walked over to Lester's body, drew his gun, shot him again and then holstered his weapon. He took another long pull on the bottle.

"Here I come!" Ernie shouted and started slowly towards the shack.

Suddenly a rock hit him in the back of the head, knocking him off balance.

He spun around and saw Jared standing inside the line of pine trees.

"Jared! But I had you killed! How?"

Jared drew in a crouch and fanned off three quick shots. All three hit Ernie between the eyes, taking out the back of his head. The bottle of whiskey dropped from his hand and broke apart on the hardpan. The outlaw's body folded and toppled over into the fire.

Jared rushed over and dragged Ernie from the flames. He looked around at the bodies. When he saw Ramsey, he knelt down to make sure he was dead, then stood up again.

"Judith?" he shouted.

"Is that you, Mr. Jared?"

"Yes, ma'am."

"In here!"

The cowboy walked quickly into the shack. He saw Judith Dalgren sitting in a chair holding a small derringer. He went to her and pulled her up into his arms. She clung to him tightly, shaking and sobbing.

"Did they kill Jace?"

"Yes."

"He tried to protect me but he couldn't. They turned on him like wild animals."

"Stay here for a while. I have to do some things out there."

"Yes. I'll wait," she said. She sat back in the chair and put the derringer in her purse.

Once outside Jared picked up the saddlebag with the money and took it over by the fire to look into it. Satisfied, he nodded and set it on the ground. Next, he stripped the outlaws of their guns and gunbelts and put them in the saddlebags on their horses.

Next, Jared went to work dragging the bodies into the pine trees, out of sight. After doing that, he gathered up old boards from the rotting shacks until he had a huge pile. He used some to stoke up the fire.

Wolves howled up in the higher hills, so he brought all the horses in close where he could watch them. The wolves would smell blood and come just before sunrise. The horses would let him know.

The next thing Jared did was to cut a bundle of soft pine branches. He laid them near the fire with several blankets over them, got the saddle from Ramsey's horse, and placed it down to be used as a pillow for Judith. He reloaded his pistol and placed three of the outlaws' rifles by the blankets. Finally, he went back into the shack for Judith. He carried her out, laid her on the blankets, and put two more over her. She was still shaking and sobbing badly.

Jared went back into the shack, got a chair and put it before the fire. He picked up a rifle and sat there.

She watched him for a while. He rolled a cigarette and smoked it, his hat pulled low and the collar of his coat pulled high against the cold. He didn't look at her but he could hear her crying. Finally, she cried herself asleep.

Jared glanced towards the hills with a worried looked on his face.

He knew they would come and that would be bad.

11.

About an hour before sunrise, the wind currents from below carried the scent of human blood up to the wolves of Wamego Falls. The alpha's green eyes glowed as it bent its snout lower to the ground to inhale the odor. It started to salivate. Spittle dripped from its jowls. The pack caught the scent too and gathered around the big leader, waiting for his command.

A feast lay a half mile below in the hardpan area where humans were.

The alpha rose to his full height, leaned into the wind and started down the mountainside at a slow canter. Its sleek, muscular body cut the wind like a knife.

Down below Judith suddenly awoke. The horses were stomping the rocky ground with their front hooves and straining to break their hobbles.

"Mr. Jared!"

Startled, Jared jumped up, sending his chair flying.

"What is it?"

"The horses."

Jared took one quick glance and ran over to his mount to get his fifty-foot lariat. He looped one end of it through the bridle of each animal, ran it over to a pine tree and tied it up. That done, he checked the hobbles to make sure they were secure.

"They're coming," Jared said, panting, as he came back to the fire.

"Who?"

"The wolves," Jared said. "They got the scent of the blood. They're coming for the bodies."

"They're going to eat them?"

"Yes."

"Poor Jace."

Jared chucked nervously. "It ain't him I'm worried about. It's us. They'll come after us first, to clear the field, then get at the bodies."

"Oh, dear," Judith fretted. "Perhaps we should go."

"It's too late. They're almost here."

"Are we in danger?"

"Pretty much so," Jared said. "Best get close to the fire."

He ran to the woodpile, grabbed an armful and tossed it into the now dying embers. In a few moments it flared and the flames lit up the surrounding area.

"There!" Judith pointed.

At first it was hard to see, then it came slowly out of the darkness and stood staring at them, hunched low to attack. It was in front of the pines where Jared had dragged the bodies. Its green eyes danced in the firelight. Its eyes were fastened on the rifle in Jared's hands as if it knew it was a threat.

"Don't move," Jared whispered. "Don't talk loud."

"Oh, God! They're doing something to the bodies," Judith whined. She started to sob. "Can't you stop them? Shoot them?"

"Not unless they come at us."

"Please do something."

"I am. I'm saving us. They're too many. Just stand still and be quiet."

Judith nodded and stood frozen in place, choking back tears. "Oh, God!" she whined.

They stood helpless as they heard the bodies being dragged away into the darkness. The two-hundred-pound alpha stood there a moment staring at them then slowly retreated backwards with a snarl. Its yellow fangs glistened in the firelight. It turned and disappeared from view. The alpha had done what it was supposed to do, protect the pack.

Judith exhaled and sighed. "Was that the leader?"

"Yes."

"He was an absolutely magnificent beast, wasn't he?"

Jared nodded. "That he was. And he could snap your neck like a twig, ma'am," Jared chuckled.

"Did you notice how the horses settled down?"

"Animals will do that when they know there's no place to run. They accept it."

"I see."

They stood by the fire until the first hint of the sun rose in the east. Jared made coffee and they had jerky and hardtack. After that, he put the saddle back on Ramsey's horse, then rolled, and tied the blankets back on the horses.

Besides Jared's and Judith's horse, the five outlaw horses and the packhorse had to be fed. Jared led them over to where winter grass poked through the snow and left them to eat and nibble at the bark of the birch trees. After that, he led them over to the stream to drink. He finally tied them in a line and put the saddlebag with the money on Mrs. Dalgren's horse.

"Can you ride, ma'am?"

"Yes," Judith said. "I'm fine now."

They left Wamego Falls and headed slowly south with the small caravan of horses tied to Judith's saddle. It began to snow and the wind picked up. Jared rode alongside her at first, keeping watch. When he saw that she was doing fine, he took the lead.

Riding into Belcher's Flats about two in the afternoon, they headed straight for the beanery in the middle of town. As they passed Dotty's Place, they gave it a glance. A man on the porch saw them and ran inside, but they kept going until they got to the beanery.

They tied up, went in and took a table by a window. They were the only people in the place. An old woman came from the kitchen and took their order.

"I'm famished," Judith said.

"You need to chomp down on a bloody steak, Mrs. Dalgren," Jared chuckled. "Get some iron in your blood."

"Yes, I think I'll just do that."

They ordered mashed potatoes, pole beans, and two rare steaks smothered in fried onions. When the food came, it was hot and steaming. They ate like hungry bears, wolfing their food, but slowed down when the apple pie and coffee came. When he was finished, Jared leaned back in his chair and rolled a cigarette.

Judith sat staring out the beanery window, watching the snowfall. Her eyes were moist again.

"Jace Ramsey?" Jared asked.

She nodded. "He tried to keep me out of harm's way. He died over it."

"They would have killed him anyway," Jared said.

She looked at Jared. "I know what you're thinking, Mr. Jared, that I was a fool for doing what I did. But Jace Ramsey was the first man to make me feel alive. I liked the way he looked at me. For the first time in my life I felt like a woman."

Judith stopped for a moment to get her handkerchief from her purse.

"Do you think he felt the same about me?" she asked, crying. "I guess I shouldn't be asking you but I need to know, Mr. Jared."

Jared looked away for a moment and hesitated, searching for words.

"Yes. He told me he had never met a woman like you and that he'd go straight to hell and back for you. He loved you that much."

"He did? Really?"

Jared nodded. "Yes, and that's a lot for an outlaw to say."

His words seemed to clear up her doubting. It was what she wanted to hear. She dried her eyes with her handkerchief and put it back in her purse, smiling.

"Do I look alright?" she asked.

"You look just fine, ma'am," Jared answered with a smile. "You never looked better."

"Thank you."

There were loud voices out on the street. Jared glanced out and saw Dotty Belcher and two men. The men were armed and they didn't look like cowboys.

"Come out here, Clay Jared! Come out an' meet yer maker, ya sonofabitch!" Dotty bellowed like an enraged bear. "Yer time has come!"

Judith glanced out the window. She looked frightened.

"Don't go out there, Mr. Jared! Please!"

"I have to, ma'am," Jared replied. "The horses and the money are out there. She's got me cornered, alright."

"Then I'll go with you."

"Best stay out of this, ma'am. It ain't gonna be pretty."

Judith pulled the derringer out of her purse. "I loaded it after I shot that horrible man back there. I have bullets."

Jared glanced at the pistol. "Alright. Put it in your coat pocket and keep a grip on it, like you're keeping your hands warm."

"Alright."

"And don't stand close. Five feet away is good," Jared explained, "and to the right. They'll be concentrating on me, not you. You'll be fine, ma'am, just relax. Take a deep breath."

Judith nodded, then inhaled and exhaled. She tried to smile.

"Aren't you afraid?" she asked.

"I'm always afraid," Jared said.

"Those were not the words I was hoping to hear, Mr. Jared."

Before Jared could reply, Dotty screamed out again.

"Get yer ass out here, Clay Jared! Or are ya hidin' behind the lady's skirt like a scared dog?"

Judith stood up and yelled back, "Miss Belcher! Can we talk before you start shooting?"

"Sure, lady, come on out and bring the yellah-belly with ya!"

"Let me go first," Judith said as Jared got up. She went out and he followed.

A small crowd had gathered. Dotty and her two gunmen stood in front, alongside each other.

The men had the cold, distant look of men who lived by the gun. One had a half sneer on his lips and the other a full scowl. Both were tall, wiry men. The brims of their black hats were tilted upward so they could better take in their surroundings. Their dark, dead, emotionless eyes were set back under wide foreheads.

They both wore guns and so did Dotty.

"Miss Belcher," Judith said. "What is it exactly that you want from us?"

"If ya have ta know, he killed two of my men and smacked me in the kisser, the bastard," Dotty growled.

"So you're angry because your two men failed to kill Mr. Jared? Is that what it's all about, Miss Belcher?"

"Never mind about that, lady. What I wanna know is, where the hell is Jace Ramsey?"

"He's dead," Judith replied.

Dotty Belcher pointed at Jared.

"Then I'm gonna kill him fer killin' Jace!"

"He didn't kill Mr. Ramsey."

"No? Who the hell did?"

"His men did," Judith replied.

Jared chuckled.

"What's so funny, mister?" the taller of the two gunmen growled.

"Her pretending to be upset about Jace Ramsey, when she and Ernie planned to kill him all along and split the money."

"You lyin' dog!" Dotty screamed. "Thet's a damn lie!"

"I saw you and Ernie talking off to the side, planning it all out," Jared said.

"Ask Ernie and the rest of 'em," Dotty sneered. "They'll say what a liar you are, Jared!"

"Ernie's dead. They're all dead. I killed Ernie, fair and square," Jared said. "And before he croaked he told me about your plan to get the money."

"Kill 'im, boys!" Dotty yelled.

The two gunmen drew. Jared beat the taller one by a bare second and fanned off a bullet into his heart. His body jerked against his partner knocking his aim off as he shot at Jared. His partner's bullet tore Jared's hat off just as Jared went into a crouch and fanned off two quick shots. They smacked into the second man's stomach and heart with a sickening thud. He danced, then twisted and fell alongside the taller gunman.

Suddenly Jared felt a bullet clip his left arm, near the elbow. He turned to see Dotty pulling the hammer back for a second shot. She never made it. Judith already had her derringer out and shot her in the heart.

For a moment the big woman looked surprised. She held a hand to her chest, then pulled it away covered with blood.

"Hell, that ain't no gun," she sneered as she turned towards Judith. "I got a real gun!"

As Dotty raised her Colt to shoot Judith, Jared fanned off a shot. It hit her between the eyes. The big woman's head snapped back and she spun sideways. A second later, she fell flat on her back on the snowy road. Her lifeless eyes stared up at the cold winter sky.

Jared looked around, his gun held at hip level. The street was now deserted except for the three bodies, Judith and him.

"Are you alright, ma'am?"

Judith looked pale but held herself steady.

"What?" she said after a moment's pause. "Oh, yes, I believe I am, Mr. Jared." She looked at the derringer for a moment as if seeing it for the first time, then slowly put it in her coat pocket. "Can we leave now?"

"Yes," Jared replied.

They untied the horses, mounted up and rode out of Belcher's Flats just as the marshal was coming up the road towards the beanery.

When they were about five miles away from town, they stopped as Judith broke down and cried.

"Oh, God! I just killed another person! What's happening to me? I've killed two human beings!"

"You had to. If you didn't kill them they would have killed you," Jared said. "That's how you have to think of it. If you don't, you won't be able to carry the weight. It'll crush the life out of you, ma'am."

She didn't seem to hear him and kept sobbing and shaking. Jared sat quietly until she was drained of emotion. It was then that she nodded and they rode on.

Jared knew she would have bad dreams. They would come to her, unexpectedly, in the night and sometimes even in the day.

Just like they did to him.

12.

Snow dogged them all the way. Twenty miles south of Belcher's Flats, they came to an old, abandoned line shack on a hill near the Kansas Pacific Railroad. The tracks were only fifty yards downhill from them. It was getting dark so they made camp for the night. Jared hobbled the horses near a tree where winter grass poked through.

The wall of the shack facing the railroad had been torn down, and it was empty except for an old wooden table with one leg missing. Jared busted it up into small pieces and started a fire. Soon they were sitting on blankets on the frozen dirt floor warming their hands while the coffee water boiled. In a few minutes they were eating hardtack and jerky and drinking bitter coffee.

Judith chuckled.

"What's so funny, ma'am?"

"Hardtack, jerky and strong, black coffee," Judith said. "I heard about such food but I never dreamed I would be eating it."

"No?"

"No. I have eaten everything from caviar to pheasant but never this."

"Someday you'll look back on this with fond memories, I suspect," Jared said.

Judith smiled. "Perhaps I will, Mr. Jared."

They heard the soulful wail of a train whistle in the distance. It came towards them getting louder, and soon they saw the light of its engine. Minutes later it sped by, blasting a path through the deep snow, sending thick plumes of cotton high into the air as it plowed its way west.

They could see the dim lights in the cars where the passengers sat reading, talking and sleeping, dressed in hats, coats and scarves, secure in their iron cocoon. Finally, the brightly lit caboose rattled by and there was only the fading sound of the engine whistle.

"Have you ever ridden in a train, Mr. Jared?"

"No, ma'am, but I've known men who robbed them."

They both laughed.

"I now own stock in that railroad down there," she said proudly.

Jared nodded. "That's good, ma'am. I'm happy for you."

They made idle talk for a while, mostly with her asking him about his life and experiences. She had been pretty much isolated from things. But not anymore. In the past few days she had gotten a big dose of reality in the harshest way. It was an experience that would last her for a lifetime.

"Christmas is not far away," Judith said. "How do you cowboys spend Christmas?"

"That depends where we are. If we're out on the range, the cook might make something special. If we're in town, we might get drunk."

Judith laughed and said, "Oh, my!"

Jared tore some boards loose from one wall of the shack and made a pile large enough to keep the fire burning throughout the night. He got extra blankets and two saddles for pillows. They bedded down close to the flames.

During the night a stray dog came sniffing around. Jared tossed it a piece of jerky. It gulped it down and curled up by the fire to sleep. In the morning, it was gone. They had breakfast and started out again, heading southeast.

Soon they began to see large groups of cattle and then cowboys. They waved to them.

"Where are you taking me, Mr. Jared?" Judith asked.

"Home, to Perryville," Jared replied.

He saw the look of relief on her face. It was red and raw from exposure to the brutal prairie wind.

"Thank you, sir," she said as if a heavy load had been lifted from her shoulders.

As they rode into town in mid-afternoon, people stared at them. They passed shops, businesses, banks and saloons. Perryville even had a small opera house. A man standing in front of a mercantile called to them. He was elegantly dressed in a fur coat and felt hat.

"Oh, my God! Mrs. Dalgren, is that you?"

They stopped and the man hurried across the street to them.

"Hello, Mr. Pearson," Judith said. The man stared questioningly at the cowboy then quickly ignored him.

"They said you had been kidnapped by the Jace Ramsey gang. It's been in all the newspapers, Mrs. Dalgren." He paused to squint suspiciously at Jared once more, and then went on. "Sorry about Mr. Dalgren. Very sad, indeed. Are you all right? Shall I call the marshal?"

Judith Dalgren laughed. "No, Mr. Pearson. I notice you are curious about my friend, Mr. Jared. He rescued me and the money from the Ramsey gang."

Suddenly Jared was okay, a fine man.

"That is just wonderful! Wonderful!" Mr. Pearson said enthusiastically. "The board of directors will be ecstatic!"

"Is the bank still open?"

"Why, yes, it is."

"Then you lead us and we'll follow," Judith smiled. She seemed to be enjoying the moment.

The bank was in the center of the sprawling cattle town. When they arrived, Mr. Pearson ran in shouting. Jared and Judith dismounted. He grabbed the saddlebag with the money and followed her into the Perryville Cattlemen's Savings and Loan.

They were met inside by customers, tellers, guards and a scholarly looking, gray-haired man whom Jared took to be the manager of the bank.

Everyone stared at them.

Judith's dress and fur coat were frayed and torn. Her skin was scorched brown by the sun and her lips were chapped. Her hair was beaten into disarray by the wind. As for Jared, his cowboy clothing was more suited to the outdoors and he was just plain dirty.

"My God, Judith," the elderly man said. "You poor soul!"

"I'm fine, Mr. Farrow," Judith said. "And I have the money."

Jared dropped the saddlebag on a nearby desk that had Mr. Pearson's nameplate on it. He stepped back as Mr. Farrow opened the saddlebag and dumped the money out on the desk. Everyone gathered around as the tellers began counting it.

It was as if Clay Jared weren't even there. He had now become the invisible man.

Jared smiled and backed away quietly to the door. Just as he reached it, Judith broke from the crowd, called and hurried up to him.

"Where are you going, Mr. Jared?" she asked.

He looked away for a moment.

"Ah, ma'am, well, I was planning to go see the marshal and let him know what happened up there at Wamego Falls. He might also want to talk to you so the law can close the book on the Ramsey gang."

"Alright, but come back when you're finished," Judith said. "Mr. Pearson said you're in for a reward."

"A reward?" Jared asked.

"Yes, five hundred dollars."

Jared nodded. "Alright. Where is the marshal's place?"

"The jail is right down the road. You can't miss it."

"Come outside a moment, ma'am," he said.

Judith followed him outside. He separated Ramsey's horse from the others and tied it to the rail then put the one she was riding in its place.

"That's Ramsey's horse, ma'am," he said. "I thought you might like to have it. Saddle and all."

She walked over to the horse and stroked its neck. It sniffed her then nuzzled her.

"He likes me."

She choked back tears.

"Yes, I see he does," Jared swung up onto his own mount and tipped his hat to Judith. "I'll be seeing you, ma'am."

"You're not coming back, are you?"

"Ah, no, ma'am, I reckon not."

"What about that reward?"

"I'll send you a wire at the bank when I find work."

"Alright," she said, her voice sounded strange, as if she was going to cry again.

"I wish you luck, ma'am." Jared said as he rode off, towing the horses.

"The same to you, cowboy!" she shouted as he rode slowly down the road.

Jared found the jailhouse to be a small clay and fieldstone building next to the stable. A sign pronounced John Stegman was marshal. He tied the horses at the rail and walked in.

An old man wearing a marshal's badge was sitting in a chair reading a penny dreadful with his feet propped up on a desk. When he saw Jared he dropped the magazine and sat up straight in the chair.

Jared noticed a wanted poster for the Jace Ramsey gang on the wall by the door. Jared took it down and laid it across the lawman's desk. It announced a five-hundred-dollar reward.

"Hello, Marshal. My name is Clay Jared. The Ramsey gang is out of business."

The marshal chuckled.

"Yeah? Who told you that, young man?" the marshal asked, as if he didn't believe Jared.

Jared sat down in a chair by the marshal's desk and told his story. When he was finished, the marshal whistled.

"An' you can prove all that?"

"Sure, easy," Jared replied. "Mrs. Dalgren is up at the bank right now. Her and the whole bank will back up my story, including Mr. Pearson and Mr. Farrow."

The marshal was hooked. Those three names sold him.

"Alright, then, here's what I'll do. You write out a statement and sign it, and I'll ask Mrs. Dalgren if it's true, being as there are no bodies to see. If it is, then the five hundred is all yours."

"I've got all their horses and gear outside," Jared said, "if you want to check them out. The saddles have their names on them. I gave Ramsey's horse to Mrs. Dalgren."

"I'll do that," Marshal Stegman said. He walked outside with Jared and checked the saddles. The marshal nodded.

"You'll have to wait a few days for that reward until the town council looks over the paperwork and all."

Jared thought about that for a moment.

"Can you give it to Mr. Pearson at the bank to hold for me until I send for it?"

"I don't see why not, sure."

They shook hands and Jared walked the horses across an empty lot to the stable.

The stable owner said, "Those are mighty fine horses ya got there, sonny. Where did ya pick them up?" Jared told the story again. "The Jace Ramsey gang, huh?"

"Yep. Mrs. Dalgren will back me up on it," Jared said.

"You want ta sell 'em, do ya?"

"Sure, all except the packhorse. How much will you offer?"

"Five hundred."

"I'll throw in the saddles and rifles if you'll make it six."

"It's a deal. Six hundred."

They sealed the bargain with a handshake. The stableman went into his office and got the money. Jared shoved it in his shirt pocket.

Jared stripped the saddlebags from the outlaw horses, tied them to the packhorse, and rode away. Five miles outside of town he stopped in a stand of pine trees.

After dismounting, Jared examined the saddlebags that belonged to Ernie, Lester, Phil and Sammy. To his surprise he found varying amounts of money in each one. It was most likely from a past robbery done while Jace Ramsey was in jail.

It came to three thousand dollars.

Jared put the money in his own saddlebag then put all the outlaws' gunbelts and guns in another saddlebag. He tied it on the packhorse but left the remaining saddlebags on the ground covered with pine needles. No one would ever find them.

Now the only things on the packhorse were the saddlebags with the guns and the food.

As Jared rode west towards Junction City, he felt good about having all that money. Now he didn't have to ride the range for a long time if he didn't want to.

But the thing was, he wanted to. It was in his blood. He was a cowboy. He would shrivel up and die if he didn't have that. He needed the range like a tree needed water. He needed all that more than he needed money.

Cowboys weren't rich but they were special, and one thing a cowboy didn't need was wealth, comfort, or possessions. A simple, routine life was the best.

Jared leaned over the saddle and patted his horse's neck.

"Thanks, old friend," he said.

Evening was closing in. He would stop at the next town and treat his old friend to a bag of oats and a rubdown. After that, he'd go to a beanery, and order another one of those big steaks smothered in onions and have a whole apple pie to himself.

Soon he'd sign on with another ranch and ride for the brand.

He would always be a cowboy. It was in his blood.

The End

Fight for the Lazy M
Red Bandana

Jack Cordell Westerns

The Gunfighter in Winter
Long Ride to Hell's Kitchen
Owl Hawks
Gunfight at Barfield Springs
Shootout at Sanctuary City
Last Days of a Gunfighter

Clay Jared Westerns

Copperhead Moon
Cowboys of the Box R
Prisoners of Brimstone Pass
Range War in C Minor
Devil Wind
Showdown at Wamego Falls

Coming Soon: Jesse Garnett Westerns

ABOUT THE AUTHOR

R. Annan is a seasoned and traveled author with many interests. As a career serviceman, he served in Korea and Vietnam. He also completed a one-year course at the Defense Language Institute at Monterey, California, and graduated from the University of South Florida with a B.A. in Art and Art History. After taking a two-year course in screenwriting at the Hollywood Scriptwriting Institute, he established The Old Time Radio Club Time Machine as both a scriptwriter and an actor.

As a young boy growing up in the city, the author never passed up a chance to see a western movie. His heroes were Buck Jones, Johnny Mack Brown, Wild Bill Elliot and John Wayne, to name a few. As an adult, he often wondered where his love of westerns came from. Perhaps it has something to do with his grandfather, John L. Annan, who was a cowboy from Helena, Montana, in days of old.

A Note from the Author

Thank you for reading my book. If you enjoyed it, would you please consider rating and reviewing it? I'd enjoy your feedback. Thank you!